**Children love sharing books.
Having a regular story time helps
encourage your child's reading.**

Going to nursery for the first time can be very
overwhelming for a young child. Nita is not sure
that she wants to go, but this delightful story
about the fun times she has, and the new friends
she meets, helps parents and children to come to
terms with this new adventure.

We hope My World™ helps you to make the
most of sharing books with your child.

Going to Nursery

Illustrations by
Amelia Rosato

First published in Great Britain 2000
This edition published in Great Britain 2001 by Egmont Children's Books Limited
a division of Egmont Holding Limited
239 Kensington High Street, London W8 6SA
Illustrated by Amelia Rosato.
Text by Laura Dollin. Designed by Mandy Norman.
With special thanks to the Brodetsky Nursery School for their help during research.
Copyright © Egmont Children's Books Limited
ISBN 0 434 80748 6
Printed in Italy
1 3 5 7 9 10 8 6 4 2

Why do I have to go to nursery?
"You'll have lots of fun there, Nita," says Mum.

But Sammy doesn't have to go to nursery.
I don't want to go there today.

Why do I have to come
to nursery?
"Look at all the fun
things to do!" says Mum.

But Mum doesn't stay for long at nursery.
I don't want to be by myself today.

Why do I have to be at nursery?
"Let's go and see what Tom's doing," the nursery lady says.

But these toys are different from my toys at home.
I wish I was at home today.

Why do I have to come
to nursery again?
I've been here before and
it's always the same.
I hang up my coat on my
own special hook,

I **play** in the sandpit,

and now I'm a cook,

. . . Build houses with Tom, get paper and glue . . .

. . . for some sticking and colouring – **so** much to do!

Red paint, blue paint, yellow paint, green,
These are the best paints I've ever seen!

Then it's time for a snack, a drink and a story . . .

Maybe I DO like nursery today!

Another day at nursery. What shall I do?
"I'm playing the tambourine," Tom says to me.

Bang! Bang! Bang! Bang! The drum is best of all!
I like it even better at nursery today.

What shall we play when we go outside?

I climb, Tom climbs, we both slide down

Pedalling *fast* on red and yellow tricycles,
I'm having *lots* of fun at nursery today!

Why do I have to go home again now?
"It's teatime," says Mum, "You'll be back tomorrow."

Today I'll take my painting home to show to Dad and Sammy.

I can't wait to go back to nursery again!

Enjoy sharing all fifteen My World™ storybooks

 Our New Baby

 On the Move

 We're Moving House

 I Don't Want To!

 We're Going Swimming

 That's Mine!

 My New Haircut

 Smile! We're Off to the Dentist

 Let's go on Holiday!

 My Visit to the Doctor

 Goodnight, Ben

 Going to Nursery

 Happy in my Nappy

 Let's Go Shopping!

 My Day at the Zoo